THE ADVENTURES OF CAVEBOY

 **READ & BLOOM BOOKS**

Agnes and Clarabelle

Agnes and Clarabelle Celebrate!

Stinky Spike the Pirate Dog

Stinky Spike and the Royal Rescue

Wallace and Grace Take the Case

Wallace and Grace and the Cupcake Caper

The Adventures of Caveboy

Caveboy Is Bored!

THE ADVENTURES OF CAVEBOY

SUDIPTA BARDHAN-QUALLEN
ILLUSTRATED BY ERIC WIGHT

BLOOMSBURY

NEW YORK LONDON OXFORD NEW DELHI SYDNEY

To my little cavebabies —S. B.-Q.

To Ethan, Abbie, Killian, Finn,
and Isla —E. W.

Text copyright © 2017 by Sudipta Bardhan-Quallen
Illustrations copyright © 2017 by Eric Wight

First published in the United States of America in August 2017
by Bloomsbury Children's Books
www.bloomsbury.com

Bloomsbury is a registered trademark of Bloomsbury Publishing Plc

For information about permission to reproduce selections from this book, write to
Permissions, Bloomsbury Children's Books, 1385 Broadway, New York, New York 10018
Bloomsbury books may be purchased for business or promotional use. For information on bulk
purchases please contact Macmillan Corporate and Premium Sales Department at
specialmarkets@macmillan.com

Library of Congress Cataloging-in-Publication Data
Names: Bardhan-Quallen, Sudipta, author.
Title: The Adventures of Caveboy / by Sudipta Bardhan-Quallen.
Description: New York : Bloomsbury USA Children's, 2017.
Summary: Caveboy loves banging his club, running really fast, and playing with his friends,
but when his club breaks, he needs to find a new one, leading him to making a new
friend and discovering his own bravery.
Identifiers: LCCN 2015036434
ISBN 978-1-61963-986-7 (hardcover) • ISBN 978-1-68119-078-5 (e-book)
Subjects: | CYAC: Cave dwellers—Fiction. | Friendship—Fiction. | Courage—Fiction. | BISAC:
JUVENILE FICTION / Readers / Chapter Books. | JUVENILE FICTION / Humorous Stories. |
JUVENILE FICTION / Social Issues /Friendship.
Classification: LCC PZ7.B25007 Ad 2016 | DDC [E]—dc23
LC record available at https://lccn.loc.gov/2015036434

Art created with Photoshop
Typeset in Chaparral Pro, Tiki Island, and House of Terror • Book design by John Candell
Printed in China by C&C Offset Printing Co., Ltd., Shenzhen, Guangdong
1 3 5 7 9 10 8 6 4 2

TABLE OF CONTENTS

CHAPTER 1
Meet Caveboy

This is Caveboy. He lives in a cave.
He likes wearing furry clothes.

He has one little sister. "Why do
I even need one sister?" Caveboy
whines.

He has one pet rock. "Just one *for
now*," Caveboy whispers.

 1

He has only one eyebrow. "All you need is one!" Caveboy shouts.

Most important, Caveboy has a club. He loves his club.

"Every caveperson should have a club," Caveboy says.

Clubs are good for thumping

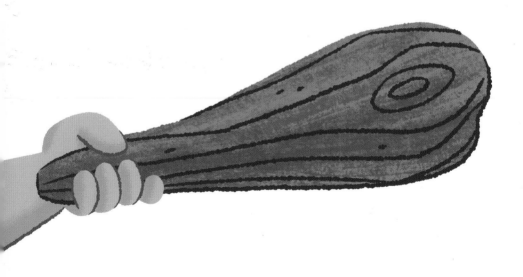

things. They are good for thumping

bushes, tree trunks, and other stuff.

They are not good for thumping

mammoths.

Clubs are good for reaching things

on high branches. They are good for

reaching flowers, fruit, and other stuff.

They are not good for reaching beehives.

There are many things that a caveperson can do with a club. But what clubs are especially good for is playing baseskull.

Caveboy loves baseskull. It is his favorite sport. Sometimes he imagines he is the greatest baseskull player in the world!

"Mama, will you play catch with me?" Caveboy asks. He holds up a pouch of skulls for Mama to use.

"Of course, Caveboy," Mama says. She ruffles his hair and takes the pouch of skulls from his hand.

Caveboy moves away until he is standing all the way back near the fern.

Mama asks, "Are you ready?" She tosses a skull up and catches it.

"Ready, Mama," Caveboy says.

Mama throws the
skull. Caveboy holds
out his hands. "I got
it!" he yells.

The skull lands on the ground.

"Try again," Mama says. She

throws another skull to Caveboy.

"I got it!" Caveboy yells. He sees

it fly through the air. He holds up his hands and jumps up, up, up.

This skull still sails over his head.

"Maybe you need more practice," Mama says.

"Ooga booga!" Caveboy says. He frowns. His eyebrow moves down low. "I do not want to practice! I just want to play."

Mama shrugs. "It is up to you, Caveboy," she answers. "I have to start hunting dinner."

"No more catching!" Caveboy
mumbles. He picks up the pouch of
skulls. "I will pitch!"

But Mama is still hunting. So
Caveboy finds Papa.

"Papa," Caveboy says, "can I pitch to you?"

Papa drops the bones he was stacking. He smiles. "That would be great," he says.

Papa holds up his club and shouts, "Ready."

He wiggles the club back and forth, getting ready to hit the skull.

Caveboy stands tall with a skull in his hands. He winds up. He throws the pitch.

The skull flies backward, all the way behind Caveboy.

"Try again," says Papa. He smiles and holds up his club.

Caveboy winds up again. He swings his arm forward and throws the pitch.

"Oops," says Papa. "We better get out of here."

When Caveboy and Papa have run far enough, Papa pants, "You need more practice."

"Ooga booga!" says Caveboy. He shakes his head. "I do not want to practice! I just want to play."

Papa shrugs. "Everyone needs to practice, Caveboy," he answers. "But it is up to you. I have to stack these bones before your mother comes back from hunting."

"No more pitching," Caveboy grumbles. He picks up his club. "I will bat!"

But Papa is still stacking. And

Mama is still hunting. So Caveboy finds Sister.

"Sister," Caveboy says, "will you pitch to me?" He holds up his club. "I am ready!"

"Did you practice?" Sister asks.

Caveboy scowls. He stomps his foot. "I do not need to practice." He taps the ground with the tip of his club. Then he raises it up again. "Just pitch."

Sister pitches the skull. Caveboy pulls his club back and then . . .

SWING! THUMP!

"Strike one!" Sister yells.

Caveboy frowns. He swings his club back and forth. He raises it up. "Throw another pitch, Sister," he says. "I will try again."

Sister winds up for a second time. Then she pitches the skull.

SWING! THUMP!

"Strike two!" Sister yells. "I think you need some more practice at batting."

Caveboy frowns again. His eyebrow comes down low again. He taps the ground with the tip of his club. He raises the club up. "Pitch," he grumbles.

"Are you sure?" Sister asks.

"JUST PITCH!" Caveboy shouts.

Sister shrugs, and then she throws the skull. Caveboy watches it leave

her hand. He watches it fly through
the air. He takes a deep breath. He
pulls his club back and then . . .

SWING! BOOM!

This time, the skull soars up, up,
up. Finally, it lands in the grass with
a soft thump.

"Ooga booga!" Sister says. "Great hit!"

WAAAAAAAH!

Caveboy cries.

Mama hears him and runs over. "What happened?" she asks.

WAAAAAAAH!

Caveboy cries again. Tears flow down his cheeks.

Now, Papa has come to Caveboy, too. "You are a wonderful batter! No one will be able to catch the skull when you hit it like that. Why are you crying?" Papa asks.

Caveboy wipes his eyes. He sniffles.

He holds up his club. It is in two pieces. "I broke something."

Mama sighs and says, "I am sorry." She gives him a hug.

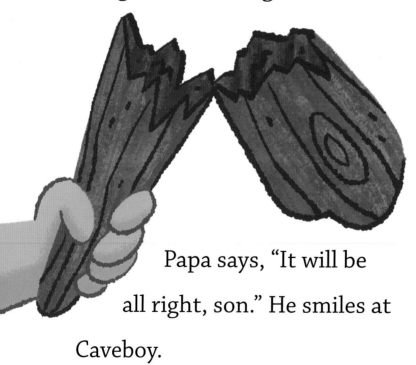

Papa says, "It will be all right, son." He smiles at Caveboy.

"Wow, maybe you practiced too much," Sister says. Caveboy scowls until she adds, "But it really was a great hit."

Caveboy drops the pieces of his club onto the ground. "It is time to stop playing baseskull with this club," he declares.

"You can still play baseskull," Papa says. He pats Caveboy's head. "We will play again tomorrow, and you will get another great hit."

"Ooga booga!" Caveboy shouts.
"That will give me time to find a new
club!"

CHAPTER 2
CAVEBOY'S CLUB

"Every caveperson should have a club," Caveboy announces. "I need to find a new club."

Papa has a club. It is very heavy.

"Papa, can I have your club?" asks Caveboy. He tries to lift it, but he cannot get it off the ground.

"This club is right for me," Papa says. "You need one that is right for you."

the grass. Caveboy inches closer. He waits for his chance. When the girl is not looking, Caveboy grabs the club and runs away.

"Ooga booga!" Caveboy says. "This is a good club!"

"Wait!" yells the girl. "You cannot take that club!"

"I am Caveboy," Caveboy shouts, "and this is the right club for me!"

"I am Mags," the girl roars, "and that is not *your* club!" Mags grabs one end of the club. "It is *my* club. Let go!"

"No!" Caveboy cries. "It is mine!" He tightens his grip on the club.

Mags is frowning. Her fingers are curled around the club. Her eyebrows are so scrunched that it looks like she has only one eyebrow.

I would not like it if someone took my club, Caveboy thinks. He lets go

of Mags's club. "I am sorry," Caveboy says. He gulps. "I should not have taken your club." Caveboy looks down at his toes. "It is just that I need a club. Every caveperson should have a club."

"You cannot just take my club," Mags says.

"I know," Caveboy mumbles. His face feels hot, and he does not look up.

"But I can help you find one," Mags adds.

Now Caveboy's head snaps up. "You will help me find a club?" he asks.

"Not any club," says Mags. "The right club for you." She smiles.

Caveboy smiles back.

Caveboy and Mags begin searching for a club. They look near the hills.

Mags points to something on the grass. "Is this a good club?" she asks.

"I do not think so," Caveboy says.

He picks it up. "Too short. It is not even as big as my arm."

"You are right," Mags says.

Caveboy and Mags search near the lake.

Mags points to something on the shore. "Is this a good club?" she asks.

"I do not think so," Caveboy says. He tries to pick it up. "Too big. I cannot hold it, even with two hands."

"You are right," says Mags.

Caveboy and Mags search near Caveboy's cave.

Mags points to something by a rock. "Is this a good club?" she asks.

"I do not think so," Caveboy says. It is covered in purple flowers. "Too fancy."

"I give up!" Caveboy yells. "I will never find the right club for me!" He stomps the ground with his foot.

"You cannot quit," Mags says. "Every caveperson needs a club."

"But I cannot find the right club. They were too heavy, too tall, too pretty, too big, too short, or too fancy."

Mags walks to the flowery club. "I like this one," she says.

"But it is too fancy!" Caveboy shouts.

"It is too fancy for *you*," Mags answers. She picks up the flowery club. "But maybe it is right for *me*."

Caveboy scratches his head. "But you already have a club. And your club is not too heavy. It is not too tall. It does not have any yellow bows on it. It is a wonderful club."

Mags twirls the flowery club. She thumps the ground with it. Then she shrugs. "I like this one more."

Caveboy crosses his arms. "Now you have two clubs," he mutters, "and I do not even have one."

Mags picks up her old club. "This

was not the right club for me," she says. "Maybe it is the right one for you?" She holds it out to Caveboy.

Caveboy takes the club from Mags's hands. He swings it up and down and all around. He thumps the ground with it. Then he grins. "I think your club is the perfect club," he announces.

"It is not *my* club," says Mags. She winks at Caveboy. "Now it is *your* club."

At first Caveboy cannot say anything. Then he smiles so hard his cheeks hurt. "Thank you, Mags," he says. "You are a good friend."

CHAPTER 3
I WiLL WiN!

Ever since Mags helped Caveboy find the perfect club, Caveboy and Mags have been best friends.

"What do friends do?" asks Mags.

Caveboy does not know. He shrugs. "We could thump things with our clubs," he says.

 47

So they thump the ground. They thump a bush. They thump a mushroom.

Then Caveboy says, "This is boring. I do not want to thump all day."

"Me neither," says Mags. She scratches her head. "What else do friends do?"

"We could play with my pet rock," Caveboy says.

They go to Caveboy's cave, where he keeps his rock collection.

"That is a nice pet rock," says Mags. "What does it do?"

Caveboy scowls. "It sits. It does not move." He puts it on the ground. "We could thump it with our clubs?" Caveboy raises his club to thump.

But Mags shakes her head. "I do not think that would be very much fun," she says.

"You are right," Caveboy says. "That is boring."

Mags taps her foot. "What else do friends do?" she asks.

Caveboy scrunches his eyebrow. "Ooga booga!" he shouts. "We could race!"

"Great idea!" Mags agrees.

"And I will win!" adds Caveboy. The thought of winning makes him grin.

But Mags does not grin. Instead, she crosses her arms and says, "I do not think so."

Caveboy shrugs. He thinks that Mags is wrong, but he does not say that.

Caveboy and Mags line up. Caveboy says, "We will race to that tree."

Mags puts her club down in the grass.

"Why did you do that?" asks Caveboy.

"It is easier to run without a club," says Mags.

Caveboy thinks of his old club. The broken club. He does not want anything to happen to his new club.

So he makes a decision. "I will never

let this club go," he says.

Mags shrugs. "If you say so," she

answers.

Caveboy says,

One ... two ... three ... GO!

Mags runs and runs. Caveboy runs

and runs. Mags jumps over a puddle

and keeps running. Caveboy tries to jump over the puddle, but his club is too heavy. He trips and falls in the mud.

"Oof!" Caveboy moans.

From the finish line, Mags shouts, "I win!"

"Not fair," yells Caveboy. "You only won because I was carrying my club. It is hard to jump over things with a club."

"Then put your club down," Mags says.

"I cannot do that!" Caveboy shouts. "I will never let this one go."

Mags shrugs. "If you say so," she says.

Caveboy says, "Come race again. This time, I will win."

"And I will win again!" Mags adds.

Caveboy shrugs. He thinks that Mags is wrong, but he does not say that.

Mags says, "We will race from here to that rock."

Caveboy looks toward the rock. There are more puddles in the way.

Mags jumps over a log and keeps running.

This time, Caveboy knows not to jump. Not with his club.

Mags runs to the left side of the woods. She is in front of Caveboy, but he smiles anyway. That's because he knows the shortcut is through the right side of the woods.

Caveboy runs and runs. He cannot see Mags. "I think I am winning," he says.

Then he hears something.

"HELP!" someone yells.

Caveboy stops running. He looks around. He cannot see anyone.

"HELP!" someone yells again. Her voice is familiar, and it is louder than before.

HELP!

But Caveboy is not scared. He has
his club.

Caveboy runs to Mags. He raises
his club high over his head. And then
he THUMPS.

"Ooga booga!" says Mags. "You
found me! You saved me!"

"That is why you should not put
your club down," Caveboy answers.

Mags gives Caveboy a big hug.
He blushes. But because Mags is his
friend, he hugs back.

The sun begins to set. The sky is getting darker. "I want to go home," Mags sniffles.

But if they leave now it means Caveboy will not get to win a race. Caveboy's eyebrow goes low. He looks down at the ground. He does not want to go home, but he does not say that.

Then his head snaps up. He grins. He says, "I have an idea!"

"What?" Mags asks.

Caveboy says, "I will race you to *your* cave. And then I will race you back to *my* cave."

Mags scratches her head. "But I will not come back to your cave today. I will stay in my own cave."

Caveboy smiles. "That just means that I will win!"

READ & BLOOM

Agnes and Clarabelle are the best of friends!

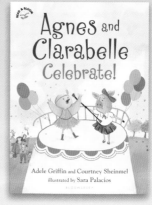

Caveboy is always ready for an adventure!

You don't want to miss these great characters! The Read & Bloom line is perfect for newly independent readers. These stories are fully illustrated and bursting with fun!

READ EVERY SERIES!

Stinky Spike can sniff his way out of any trouble!

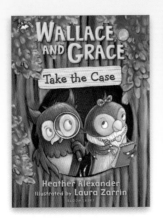

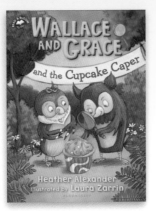

Wallace and Grace are owl detectives who solve mysteries!

 www.bloomsbury.com • Twitter: BloomsburyKids • Facebook: KidsBloomsbury

SUDIPTA BARDHAN-QUALLEN lives in New Jersey with her cavefamily—three cavekids and one cavehusband. She cannot hit baseskulls, hunt saber-tooth tigers, or scare away spiders, but she is very good at reading, traveling, and shopping for shoes. Sudipta is the award-winning author of over forty books for children, including *Duck, Duck, Moose!*, *Tyrannosaurus Wrecks!*, and *Chicks Run Wild*.

sudipta.com

ERIC WIGHT spends a lot of time in his cave making books for children, including the Frankie Pickle and Magic Shop series. When he was a kid, he had a unibrow just like Caveboy. He lives with his wife and herd of children in Chalfont, Pennsylvania.

ericwight.com